Chirpy

The Girl of the Sun

Arno Bo lives with his two daughters in Holland. This is his second book to be published by Bloomsbury Children's Books. The first is called *I Must Tell You Something* – the tragic but heart-warming story of his family, coping with life after a car accident.

Chirpy

The Girl of the Sun

By Arno Bo

Bloomsbury

First Published in Great Britain in 1997
Bloomsbury Publishing Plc, 38 Soho Square, London W1V 5DF

The moral right of the author has been asserted
A CIP catalogue record of this book is available from the
British Library

ISBN 0 7475 2529 3

Printed in England by Clays Ltd, St Ives plc

10 9 8 7 6 5 4 3 2 1

Chirpy lives in a country where Queen's Day and Liberation Day are in one week, in the middle of spring.

But then again, in other countries, spring is not in April at all. And you know, I don't think it really matters, do you? Because Chirpy's story is about the kind of love that can bridge any place or time.

So I hope you'll discover that along with her.

Arno

For Phoebe

When I'm in thought
you have to call three times
before I hear you.

You asked when I'd write
about the sun who was lonely.

CHAPTER
ONE

Sweet Soldiers

CHIRPY IS going to bed. She watches the sun go out of sight and says 'Goodnight.'

Not out loud, mind. If she talks to the sun out loud, Dad will say 'Don't be daft.'

The sun can't answer, he can only *be*. And Chirpy doesn't *want* an answer; she's too shy. She's so shy that she likes the darkness. That's why she says 'Goodnight' to the sun.

At night nobody sees her and nobody says she's daft.

She's already asleep, all curled up. What a pity you're not awake when you sleep. How then can you enjoy it?

Suddenly she's awake after all, because someone is calling. It sounds so sad that she feels it in her stomach.

It's not a dream. Chirpy's eyes are wide open. She'd like to go on sleeping, but it sounds as if a baby is crying, as if a baby is calling her.

She's going to have a look.

It's dark on the landing – good. Chirpy knows exactly where to walk and she's moving on tiptoes.

Perhaps it's the middle of the night. Is Dad asleep yet? She peeps into his room and can hear him breathing.

Next the guest-room, the study, more stairs, the attic ... There she realizes the sounds are coming from outside. From the neighbours? It would be an awful shame if there wasn't a baby.

She goes back to her room and opens the window. How mournful is that voice in the night.

But she can't see anyone and nothing is moving. She gets back into bed.

When the sun comes back, he sees a pale little girl getting ready for school – she hasn't slept well.

'Get a move on!' her father says.

Her coat isn't buttoned, her laces aren't tied, she hasn't brushed her teeth, she forgets her bag ...

'If you're late, it's your own fault,' Dad shouts. 'It's twenty-five past!'

And when Chirpy is late, she's more afraid than ever to go in. They will all be looking at her.

The sun is shining in her eyes, she blinks ... and falls. Not very hard, but the sun is shocked: is it his fault? He didn't mean to, he doesn't mean anything, he can only shine and see, except of course when a cloud gets in the way.

Chirpy is not crying, because Dad would say 'Stop snivelling.'

And that's crazy, the sun thinks, tell your father that he's being daft himself! What else is crying for?

Chirpy is glad that another day has passed by. 'Goodnight,' she says again to the sun.

He's already gone.

She has cold feet and asks for a hot-water bottle, but Dad says 'Ridiculous! A hot-water bottle in April!'

He hasn't time to make one, or he doesn't feel like it.

Chirpy is afraid she'll never be able to fall asleep with such cold feet, but she curls up extra tightly and sleeps pretty soon.

Until she wakes up in the dark again. That baby! Is Chirpy losing her mind or what? She knows there isn't a baby but she also knows somebody is calling.

Better take a look.

The floor is cold and her feet had just warmed up. Once more she searches the whole house, which is pitch dark.

What would she do if she did find a baby? Not say a word to Dad. Keep it in the attic and look after it, with hot milk, warm clothes, always have it on her lap, always give it a hot-water bottle, cuddling it, talking softly ...

Then, seeing the moon, Chirpy remembers the sounds came from outside.

This time she's not going back to bed, she puts her winter coat on, turns the key of the front door, puts the rope through the letter box and goes outside. There's nobody there, no dogs, and the birds are silent too.

Pretty, Chirpy thinks, waving to the moon – not shy at all.

She tries to count the stars.

At that moment, the crying comes closer. She feels something against her legs and wants to run away, but now she sees it's a cat. Can cats cry?

'What's wrong?' Chirpy says. 'Oh, you're looking for a girlfriend! To cuddle, I suppose. If only *I* were a cat, eh?'

She holds him on her lap, out there on the pavement, in the middle of the night, and she'd like to stay there. But the cat doesn't have the patience for that. He goes on with his search.

Chirpy thinks did I leave the door open?

She shivers and runs back. Yes, the rope is in the

letter-box. She slips inside and closes the door softly behind her, but she forgets to turn the key.

In the morning she wakes up with Dad screaming 'Who's unlocked the door? Has there been a burglar?'

He walks up and down, to see if everything is still there: money, the CD-player, the video-recorder ...

'Nothing's been stolen.'

Chirpy is silent. She's late for school again. And during playtime she falls asleep, in a corner behind the bike shed – a spot in the shade. Nobody looks for her. Nobody misses her. She lies there like a baby, with her mouth open, until school is out.

Dreamily, she walks along the pavement. Dreamily, she crosses the street. There aren't any cars, only a cyclist, who almost rides into her.

Outside her house she sees the cat again. 'Remember me?'

He stops but looks away.

'What's your name?'

Slowly he comes closer.

'You know what? I'll just call you Baby.'

He pauses again.

'Come on, Baby. Are you shy? Doesn't matter. You needn't be shy with me.'

Baby walks past, stops once more and is off into

the neighbours' garden.

The rest of the afternoon, Chirpy plays in her room, with her dolls and building blocks.

At dinner, Dad asks 'Had a good day at school?'

'Yes,' Chirpy says.

'Can you read and write now?'

Chirpy shakes her head.

'Do you try your best?'

Chirpy nods.

'Well,' says Dad, 'I don't get it.'

He takes the Radio Times and asks 'What does it say here?'

She says: 'Television.'

'No, goose, it says "Friday". That's today, understand?'

Chirpy's throat is aching and she says 'I want some water.'

'Ask for it properly.'

'Please, may I have some water, sir?'

He laughs loudly, leafs through the Radio Times and says 'You watch Newsround. It might make you a bit smarter.'

Chirpy would rather play a game but she watches *the News* and sees soldiers.

'Are they dressed up?' she asks.

Dad shakes his head.

'Are they shoot-soldiers?'

'You bet.'

'Are there any sweet soldiers too?'

'Yes. They help out when there's been a disaster.'

'Like what?'

'Like floods or a forest fire or an earthquake ...'

'Oh,' says Chirpy. 'Can they go and see Mum in the Home?'

'No love.'

She thinks for a long time and asks 'Will there be a war here?'

'Nah,' says Dad.

Then Chirpy sees that some soldiers are lying on the ground and she asks 'Is life going to die too?'

'No no, silly girl.'

'Never?'

Dad sighs and says 'When the sun stops shining.'

Chirpy looks at the television and thinks when I see in the News that the sun has fallen down, I'll ... What? She doesn't know. Not even when she thinks hard.

In fact, she'd like to ask Dad, let's play a game? But she doesn't dare.

She says 'Spain is in France, isn't it?'

And she doesn't even know *why* she says it.

CHAPTER
TWO

Heavenly

THAT NIGHT, Chirpy hears Baby calling again.

She opens her window and says 'Why don't you go home? Or don't you *have* a home? Then come and sit on my lap tomorrow, OK?'

Baby stays still.

It's already 'tomorrow', a Saturday.

Dad sleeps late. Then he has coffee and goes shopping.

'Are you coming?' he always asks.

Chirpy never goes. On sunny days she does some knitting, drawing, building, she does jigsaws, she plays school with a strict teacher, house with a strict father, shop with lots of sweets, hospital with patients who are horribly ill, she sharpens her pencils, looks at the pictures in her books, tidies the house: dusting, hoovering, sweeping, she does the dishes without dropping anything, she waters the plants without spilling anything, folds the laundry from the drier, lays the table and plays all kinds of games on her own, especially Ludo. She's crazy about that and she always loses – on her own. So she rants and raves and stamps her feet – alone. Or she flings the game across the room. Then she has to find the poor little creatures and take them to hospital, to the meanest doctor in the country, so that they have to be comforted, because they don't have a father or mother.

That's how busy Chirpy is on a sunny day.

On a cloudy day she goes outside. Not to cycle or roller-skate – she would be laughed at – but to walk and look at the trees, animals, flowers and clouds.

When she stays away all afternoon, Dad asks 'Where on earth have you been?'

'I can't remember.'

'Don't be cheeky!'

But often she truly can't remember. Just somewhere.

'As long as you look out for kidnappers,' Dad says.

'And for shoot-soldiers,' Chirpy says. 'And for disasters. Then I'll hurry home.'

Today is a cloudy day and the clouds are so thick and dark that Chirpy dares to go farther away. She's not afraid of thunder and lightning, only of the sunlight.

She chooses the paths in the big park, where motorbikes are not allowed. She looks at the new leaves on the trees, at the birds carrying twigs in their beaks, at people out walking with dogs and children, but mostly she looks at the flowers, which have just come out.

The dandelions are so yellow that they make her happy. And the daisies are such duckies ... What a shame they stay closed when it's cloudy.

Suddenly Chirpy spots a field that is all blue, a light purplish blue. It looks like a blanket for a giant's picnic.

Going closer, she sees they are flowers, so many that she can hardly see the grass. Chirpy lies on her stomach to feel them.

So this is heaven, she thinks, this is sky-blue.

She'd like to stay here for ever, but somebody is coming. She pretends she can't hear or see anything, only the colour that is warming her, but she feels somebody coming closer.

'Speedwell,' says a voice.

Chirpy keeps quiet.

Someone lies down right beside her and says 'They will be mown soon.'

It's a boy and luckily he's not very big.

Chirpy never talks to people, but now she says 'Speedwell?'

The boy is stroking the flowers and says 'Didn't you know? And my name is Boldy.'

Chirpy still has her eyes closed and asks: 'Mown?'

'Yeah, by the council gardeners.'

He makes the sounds of a big mowing machine.

Chirpy knows exactly what he means. When a monster machine like that appears, she stays indoors.

'But they grow back soon,' the boy says. 'Just like the daisies.'

For a while it's so quiet that they can hear the ants move.

Still, Chirpy doesn't forget there is somebody beside her and she says 'Boldy?'

'Yes. It's really Baldwin, but they say I'm as bold as brass.'

Chirpy jumps up and Boldy likes that.

She wants to run away but the colour of the speedwell is so lovely that she stays, and by accident she says 'Magic blue.'

'Yes,' says Boldy, 'it's called lilac.'

'Lilac?'

'Just wait for the sun to shine on it.'

Chirpy looks at the clouds. They've brightened a little.

The sun himself is invisible – *behind* the clouds –

there he is so alone that he's almost jealous of Chirpy, who's talking to Boldy as if she's not shy at all.

Clouds take no notice of the sun. They glide by and blot him out. But the wind is there too. It plays with the clouds as if it owns the sky.

All at once it's blown a little gap, through which the sun is shining on the speedwell. Now Chirpy sees what lilac colour is, not purple and not blue, but lilac! It's so beautiful that she doesn't run from the sun. She keeps jumping aside, though, into the shade.

'Yes!' Boldy calls. 'Nice game!'

He's jumping aside too and it looks like a dance, on the speedwell field.

There are new gaps in the clouds and the sun is gleaming down, until it's too much for Chirpy. Out of breath she dashes away.

She runs without looking and falls heavily on her knee. It hurts and it's bleeding, but she doesn't ask for a bandage, she goes straight to her room, locks the door and draws the curtains.

That night Chirpy sleeps so deeply that she doesn't hear Baby calling.

CHAPTER
THREE

Hello Chirp

WHEN CHIRPY wakes up, her pyjamas are sticking to the blood on her knee. The blood has dried and the trouser leg has red stains. Chirpy can stand a lot of pain, but when she pulls at the trousers, she cries out.

That gives her another scare, because it's Sunday and Dad sleeps extra late. She can do what she likes, as long as she doesn't make a sound.

She waits for him to storm out of his room. Must she wait for him all morning? In these dirty pyjamas? She tries to pull one more time. No use. And what if Dad is going to pull? She mustn't think of that. Perhaps she should cut the trousers up. And throw them away. Perhaps he wouldn't notice. He never notices anything, only when things go wrong. But she's cold as it is.

Well, better lay the table first and then play hospital again, which takes a long time, with her bad knee and everything. The doctor does it all wrong, because he's wearing sunglasses.

'Hello, girl,' Dad says at midday.

'Hello, Dad,' Chirpy says as cheerfully as possible.

He asks 'Still not dressed?'

'No, I was um ... I was a bit lazy.'

'What? You've never been *lazy* before.'

'And uh ... My trousers were a bit stuck.'

Dad roars with laughter and says 'What did you dream about this time?'

'Oh, nothing.'

'What's wrong with your trousers?'

'Oh, I just fell and there's blood on my knee.'

'Fell out of bed?' Dad says. 'Let's have a look.'

'Don't pull,' says Chirpy.

'But I need to look, don't I?'

'Won't you pull at it then?'

'No, no.'

'Honest?'

'Honest.'

Dad is holding the pyjama leg and now he gives a hard jerk.

It feels as if he's pulled the knee off her leg. Her eyes are full of tears. A dark crust is stuck to the pyjamas.

Dad is upset himself. 'Sorry,' he says. 'I didn't know it was so bad. I didn't warn you, on purpose, so as not to frighten you. I thought: a quick tug and off it comes.'

Chirpy doesn't look at him. She'd like to hit him and that frightens her even more.

There's a hole in her knee. It's bleeding heavily again and Dad puts a big bandage on it.

'What a fuss,' he says. 'Want some sweets?'

Chirpy nods.

'Here, have a handful.'

A handful? She's never had more than one.

It helps against the pain but not against the shock, nor against the anger. He *said* he wouldn't pull!

She holds her tongue and hurries to her room.

There, she flings a doll on the floor, rings the hospital and says 'Poor thing, have you had an accident? Do cry, love, I'll make you all better. Come on my lap, there ... Careful eh, *very* careful ... What a fuss. I'm sorry, I'll never do it again. You can cry, you know. So cry!'

In the afternoon it begins to rain. Dad is doing his best to make her comfortable, perhaps to make it up.

'Let's play ball,' he says.

'Indoors?' Chirpy asks.

That was never allowed before.

Dad stands far away and she drops the ball every time.

Dad comes a step closer.

The ball still slips through her hands.

Closer.

Again the ball rolls on the floor.

Now they are so close to each other that they needn't throw at all, they can just pass the ball.

Dad gives up and says 'We'll practise some other time.'

He picks up the Radio Times.

Chirpy wants to be nice too and asks 'Would you like a cake?'

'No thanks,' says Dad.

'I can make nice cakes.'

'No, I've just had coffee.'

'Oh,' says Chirpy. 'OK.'

She goes to her room and looks out of the window. The sky is still dark.

How's Baby doing? she wonders. And Boldy and the speedwell ... She'd like to go out but it's raining really hard now.

She takes a large sheet of paper, puts it on the floor and starts painting. Before she knows it, she's painted the sun. He's yellow with lilac. He peeps curiously and shyly between two thunderclouds. Quickly she paints a very tall tree. The branches reach the sun, who keeps looking.

'Hello,' Chirpy says.

She's warm with the work.

In the tree are a hundred sparrows and their tiny beaks are all open – they are chirping. She forgets where she is and cheeps a bit too.

It's getting lighter outside. The rain is over.

She puts her coat on, forgets to say goodbye to Dad and goes out. Her knee still hurts and she has to walk slowly.

On her way to the speedwell she hears a cry 'Dead!'

In the bushes she sees somebody falling. She wants to run away, but her legs refuse.

'Help!' somebody shouts.

'What's the matter?' Chirpy asks.

She goes to the bushes and sees it's Boldy.

'War!' he calls. 'I'm a soldier!'

Chirpy looks about. 'A shoot-soldier?'

'Yes, they've pinched my gun.'

'Who?'

'The enemy,' Boldy says. 'Where's your gun?'

'I haven't got a gun.'

'Go and get one, quick!'

'No, no,' Chirpy says. 'I um ... I'm a help-soldier.'

She looks about again. What's that rustling?

There's a bang.

'A cannon!' Boldy says. 'We've got to flee, help!'

He groans and cowers.

'How then?' Chirpy asks.

'I don't know. You're a help-soldier, aren't you? Quick, the enemy is coming ...'

'Why are you a *shoot*-soldier then?' Chirpy asks.

'Eh ... I was scared!'

'Me too,' says Chirpy. 'That's why I'm a help-soldier.'

For a moment Boldy is still. Then he is squirming with pain.

'A bullet! There's a bullet in my arm!'

'Get it out,' Chirpy says.

'I don't dare.'

'Show me ...'

'Don't touch it,' Boldy says.

'No.'

'Honest?'

'Honest.'

Cautiously, Boldy sits up. One arm is limp.

'Where then?' Chirpy asks.

'Well, here.'

He points to the spot, at the top of his arm.

'I see,' says Chirpy.

'You've got to operate.'

'Yes, I can, in the hospital.'

'No, here!' Boldy says. 'Now!'

'No, in the hospital.'

'Nah,' says Boldy, 'then I'll quit.'

He gets up and walks away.

'The enemy!' Chirpy shouts.

Boldy stops, thinks and comes back. He's looking for something on the ground. His arm is still limp.

'The bullet,' he says suddenly. 'It went right through my arm. So you don't have to operate, just put a bandage on.'

He's holding a pebble.

'No,' Chirpy says. 'It's not real any more.'

Boldy looks at her and says 'Too bad. Cheerio.'

His bike is against a tree, where the enemy was, and Chirpy watches how he jumps on to the saddle and rides off in one go.

She forgets to go and look at the speedwell and walks home. Her head is full of thoughts and she can deal with only one of them at a time. She doesn't like thinking very much.

At home she asks 'Can I ride my bike in the garden?'

'Why?' says Dad.

'Just to cycle – very carefully.'

'I mean,' he says, 'why in the garden?'

25

It's a very big garden and she has a small bike. She always rides from the shed to the birch tree and then to the house, again and again, but only if Dad is not at home. And if she doesn't crash. When someone is watching, for example in the street, she always crashes.

The sun peeks in through a corner – *Hello Chirp* – and tries hard to come closer, in the shade, but no matter how far he shines, he'll never reach the dark.

CHAPTER
FOUR

Why?

IT'S MONDAY morning. Dad is going to work and Chirpy has to leave for school.

'Come on,' Dad says. 'Finish your toast.'

'I'm not hungry.'

'Suit yourself.'

'I don't feel so well,' Chirpy says.

'Ah, you say that every morning. You just hate school. Hurry, brush your teeth.'

Chirpy says 'I'm too tired.'

'No, you'll be fine. I'm off to the office and if you don't hurry, we'll both be late. Brush your teeth!'

'Please, stay at home,' Chirpy says.

'ME? And who will pay for our food, our house, the clothes, the bikes ...'

'Well, with money.'

'And where do we get the money from?'

'Buy it in the bank.'

'Yes,' Dad says, 'and *I'm* the one who has to earn

that money in the bank. Haven't you brushed your teeth yet?'

'What if I'm ill?' Chirpy says.

'Really ill?'

'Dead ill, by a bullet, from a shoot-soldier ...'

'Then I'd stay at home,' Dad says.

'Honest?'

'Honest.'

'But won't you do what you did with my pyjama leg?'

Dad stops with the car keys in his hands.

'No,' he says. 'I'd ask Gran and Grandad to come.'

'Good,' says Chirpy.

Dumb, thinks the sun.

Dad works till five o'clock, so after school Chirpy is alone for a while. She used to like that, but today it's different. She'd like to play ball with Dad again.

First she rides her bike. Then she looks out of the kitchen window. Baby is strolling along the pavement. He's watching the birds, which fly up and down building their nests. When a bird sits on the ground for a second, Baby leaps at it – too late. What a good thing that birds can fly.

Near the window Baby stops. He looks at Chirpy, with his gleaming eyes, and walks on.

Chirpy feels like a walk too, but it's rather sunny. She hangs about, takes all the children from the dolls' house for a walk, counts her marbles, which she never plays marbles with, puts the colours together and makes them tinkle in the alley. Then she uses a strip of cardboard to stop the marbles and when she takes it away again, all the marbles roll at a jingling speed down the little stairs. Again and again, they jingle down the alley.

When Dad is watching TV, this game drives him mad. When he's reading the paper, the marbles drive him mad too. And when he's on the phone ... Oh well, you can say there's always something driving him mad.

The marbles alley was a present from Mum, who now lives on the other side of the country, in that Home with the other people, where it's nice all right but where you can't visit.

It's four o'clock. Chirpy lays the table and looks outside again. She'd really like to know where Baby was going.

Mum also gave her a pair of sunglasses, with a sun-hat. But when she wears them, everybody laughs at her. On the hat is a long ribbon and a big, white rose, made of silk.

Sometimes she wears it in her room, to be a lady

who is so lovely that everybody wants to marry her.

Sometimes she forgets to take it off when Dad comes home. Then he says 'Don't be silly.'

The sun is trying to shine a bit less, to draw Chirpy outside. He wants her to come and pick flowers. The fields are full of flowers, asking to be picked.

Of course the sun can't shine less, but there are fleecy clouds now and he can peep through safely.

For one more second, Chirpy hesitates. Then she goes out, wearing her coat.

Under some of the trees it is shady, but the leaves of other trees are still too small and that's where the most beautiful flowers grow, in the light.

For brief moments, Chirpy steps out of the shade, going from one tree to another, and by the time she's on her way home with a big bunch of flowers, the sun has hidden some light in the flowers. So she's taking that home by accident.

Near the house, Chirpy has to cross the bike track. She looks out carefully, but a motorbike comes along so fast and makes such a noise that Chirpy stops dead in the middle of the path – as if pinned to the ground.

Has the driver seen her? She's so small! So long as she doesn't move now, he'll go right past her. She mustn't jump with fright ...

Like a wild animal he seems to charge. Step on the brakes!

He swerves, bangs against the edge of the pavement and thunders past.

He's gone. Nothing has happened. Chirpy hasn't been hit, only by the noise.

Now it grows extra still. Chirpy hasn't moved yet. She's even holding the flowers.

In the silence, somebody yells: 'Prat! Idiot! Nitwit! Limpsock! Cowball!'

It's Boldy. He's high up in the chestnut tree and shouts after the motorbike 'Murderer! I'll call the police!'

Chirpy jumps on the pavement and Boldy climbs down. 'Did he hit you?'

Chirpy shakes her head.

'Are you paralyzed?'

Chirpy nods.

'Can you talk?'

She nods.

'I'll carry you. All right?'

She shakes her head.

'I *want* to carry you,' Boldy says.

Chirpy starts trembling.

'What's up? Are you cold? Do you want to go to the hospital?'

Chirpy says 'Home.' And she looks at the

31

flowers in her hand.

'OK,' says Boldy. 'Cheerio.'

Slowly, thinking, Chirpy walks home. There she has time to recover. One by one she puts the flowers in a vase.

To the flowers she talks with soft words, but at the back of her mind, she hears Boldy's words, the crazy ones, which she likes at the same time.

Good, the sun thinks, looking inside – he's *very* curious.

It's a beautiful arrangement, with pink, yellow, white, blue, purple and lilac. Chirpy puts it on the dining table, between the plates. Now it's all right if Dad comes home. What a pity she can't peel potatoes. She tried once and got a deep cut in her thumb.

Dad often brings pizzas, and Chinese meals and things, but Chirpy likes potatoes much better.

When Dad comes home, he's tired. Chirpy has to do exactly as he says, or else he'll go wild. Actually, he looks so tired that she feels sorry. Actually, he looks kind of sweet too, when she takes a very good look. Which she doesn't dare, unless his eyes are closed.

He takes a can from the fridge and drinks it. Then he takes a dish from the fridge and puts it in the microwave.

Chirpy sees him looking at the flowers but he doesn't say anything and Chirpy is silent as well. She's thinking hard again. It has to do with the motorbike, with those things Boldy said, and doing jigsaws after dinner, she gets angry at the pieces that don't fit.

'Can I dry the dishes?' she asks Dad.

'If you don't drop anything,' he says.

Chirpy has never dropped anything before, but when Dad splashes some soapsuds in her face – by accident – she feels like hurling a plate at him. Which she doesn't do.

What a shame, thinks the sun, who's in a crazy mood.

After washing up, Chirpy is afraid to invite Dad for a game. He lies on the couch, until it's Chirpy's bedtime. In the meantime she has felt so strange, as if she's two people, as if someone else is thinking *for* her – someone she doesn't know yet.

The sun is almost gone, he's only a line above the horizon now, and it seems he gives Chirpy a wink.

She's on the stairs and can just see him through the fanlight. For a moment she's blinded. Then, when she opens her eyes again, the sun is gone. Only the sky is still pink. She'd like to say something, a bit more than 'Goodnight', for example, 'Thanks for the wink' or 'See you tomorrow ...' But it's too late.

Mostly, Chirpy goes upstairs alone, brushes her teeth alone and waits for Dad to come and kiss her goodnight. Now she stops, turns round and cries 'Idiot! Cowboy! Wimpwit! Nitsock!'

She cries it to the room, where Dad is still lying on the couch.

He looks about. Is that Chirpy's voice? *His* Chirpy's voice?

He thinks: I must have dozed off – it was a weird dream.

Chirpy doesn't know what is happening herself. She cries again. 'Twitball!'

Dad thinks *now* I'm awake, aren't I?

He gets up, runs to the door, pulls it open and gazes upwards.

There's Chirpy, half-way up the stairs.

Dad is stunned and Chirpy is just standing there.

At last he asks 'What's going on?'

She looks at the pink light and says 'I want *Mum* to put me to bed.'

Dad swallows and his eyes grow big.

'But sweetheart, you know Mum is very far away?'

'Sure!' says Chirpy. 'On the other side of the country, in a far too big house, with far too many people, where I can't go and stay!'

Then she asks something she's never asked before 'Why?'

Dad sighs. He sits down on a step of the stairs and sighs again. 'Because Mum is *too* sweet and *too* good.'

'For what?'

'Well, for the world.'

'Why?'

'Because the world is so busy, and difficult, and sometimes mean.'

Chirpy nods. '*Very* mean.'

'And Mum can't cope with that.'

'Never?'

'I don't know,' Dad says.

'Will she never come and live with us?'

'I really don't know.'

'But I want Mum to put me to bed.'

'No,' Dad says. 'Come on.'

He takes her hand.

Lie down and stay with me for a while, Chirpy would like to ask, but she doesn't.

She'd like to ask so much more that she can't sleep. It's just as if she has slept all her life and is now waking up.

On her pillow case are red dots. She counts them: ninety-eight, ninety-nine, one hundred, two hundred, three hundred ...

After that she tidies her wardrobe, hoping to hear Baby's calls.

She opens the window and leans outside.

Finally, when she still can't sleep, she thinks I'll go and find Baby.

In Dad's study the lights are on, but Chirpy moves softly and she knows exactly which step creaks.

Opening the front door, she is doubly careful, so careful that she forgets to put the rope through the letter-box.

As there is a thick cloud in front of the moon, it's pitch dark outside, and when Chirpy feels something against her leg, she is startled.

'Oh, it's you,' she says to Baby. 'I didn't hear you calling. Come for a walk?'

They walk to the speedwell, of course. It's Chirpy's favourite spot now.

'Do you want to sit on my lap?' she asks Baby.

He lays his head on her legs and this time Chirpy does fall asleep, until the cold wakes her up.

'Ow, I'm going home.'

She gives Baby a hug and says 'Bye bye.'

But Baby comes along too.

'All right,' Chirpy says, 'as long as you keep quiet.'

At the front door, he miaows loudly.

'What's the matter? Sshh ... Do you want to come inside? I'd like that too. You could sleep on my bed ... I wish Dad would let you.'

Meanwhile she's feeling at the letter-box for the rope. Hey, what's happened to the rope?

'Oh Baby, something's gone wrong. I can't get in!'

Baby is scratching the door and looks at the bell.

'Ring the bell?' says Chirpy. 'Oh no, I can't, I don't dare. Dad's asleep. It's the middle of the night. Or do you think it's almost morning?'

She looks at the sky. There's no trace of light yet. How long will she have to wait? And where? She's so cold. She can't lie on the pavement, can she? Nor on the grass, it's damp with dew.

For the first time in her life, Chirpy longs for the sunshine.

Perhaps she ought to go to the police. No, Dad wouldn't like that either.

Suddenly Baby walks away. He keeps looking over his shoulder, pauses, comes back and brushes against Chirpy's legs. Again he walks away, looks back and stops.

'Do you want me to come?' Chirpy asks. 'Where?'

Baby is waiting and waiting, till she follows him,

past the park, into another street, and Chirpy is very tired indeed.

'What *are* you doing?'

Baby has stopped outside a shed in a back garden.

'What's this? Who lives here?'

He rubs his back against the door.

'Can I sleep here?' Chirpy asks.

She looks around. There are no lights. She shivers with cold and opens the door of the shed. How did Baby know it wasn't locked?

In the shed are bikes, boxes, pots of paint, tools for the garden and an armchair with a rug.

'Oh,' Chirpy says, 'is this your little place? Can I borrow it?'

Baby jumps on the chair and lies in the middle of the rug. Chirpy picks him up, crawls on the chair herself, and with Baby lying on top of her, falls asleep once more.

She dreams that she's lying in a bird's nest, high in the chestnut tree. It's lovely to rock in the wind. But high in the tree come the first rays of the sun, right on her face.

Chirpy wakes up when her nose is itching. She sneezes, looks through the window of the shed and says 'Oh no, it's daylight!'

It feels as if she's been asleep for only an hour.

Baby jumps off her lap and slips out. Chirpy feels like running too, but she has a headache and a sore back – it was not really a nice bed after all.

When she arrives home again, Dad is not yet up. What a good thing the sun woke her so early.

She waits a little while, to pull herself together, then she rings the bell. She has to ring hard three times before Dad opens the door, in his pyjamas. His hair is all tousled and his eyes are half closed.

'What the heck ...' he says.

And he forgets to let her in.

'I uh ...' Chirpy says. 'Well you know – because you see – I mean there was – and then um – so I mean ...'

Dad rubs his eyes. 'Pardon?'

Chirpy says 'So I was awake or something, anyway, and I went outside for a sec or something and the door sort of shut, you see ...'

'I see?' Dad shouts. 'At a quarter past six in the morning?'

'Look, you know, I needed to pee so then I was a bit confused or something and anyway, the wrong door was open and well, I was sort of outside.'

She sneezes and shivers again.

'Terrific!' Dad says. 'Do you want to stay there?'

'No,' says Chirpy.

39

She steps into the hall and says 'What about school?'

'Certainly you're going to school, but not at a six a.m! Have another try at finding your bed.'

She falls asleep again and dreams that she's climbing out of the window.

CHAPTER
FIVE

Afraid

AT SCHOOL everything goes wrong.

The teacher shakes her head and says 'My girl, my girl ...'

Chirpy thinks deeply and says 'I don't feel very well.'

'No,' says the teacher, 'I can see that. Why?'

'Oh, I don't know.'

'What's the matter?'

'Oh, nothing, Miss.'

'How's your father?'

'Oh, I don't know. I mean, fine, Miss.'

And your mother? the teacher would like to ask.

But people never ask about Chirpy's mother.

After dinner Chirpy sneezes eight times.

'There you are,' Dad says, 'caught a cold. I suppose you'll be ill on Queen's Day. Typical. Better get to bed early.'

Chirpy falls asleep immediately. But her nose becomes all stuffed up, so that she can't breathe, and that makes her have horrible dreams, about fires and wars and a pit with Mum in it, a deep pit full of mud.

Chirpy is on the edge of the pit and says 'Please come. I'll help you. Hold on. Take my hand. You're safe with me ...'

'I can't,' Mum says. 'You'd fall in the pit too.'

Chirpy is too small to pull, but she cries 'Do try, I've got magic strength, you have to dare, you have to believe me, hold on!'

At this moment Dad comes in.

'Don't shout like that. What's the matter?'

Chirpy wakes up with a fright and she can't speak.

'Hush,' Dad says. 'Did you have a nasty dream? Never mind. Nothing happened. See? You're in bed. Do you know what time it is?'

'No,' says Chirpy.

'Two o'clock.'

'Is it almost morning then?'

'No,' Dad says. 'Thank God. We can sleep for a nice long time.'

'I *can't* sleep any more.'

'Yes, you can ...'

'I'll dream again!' Chirpy says.

'Go and have a pee,' Dad says. 'I'll get something for your nose.'

Chirpy has a big pee. Then her bed is more comfy than ever.

Dad puts something under her nose and says 'Smell this. What do you think it is?'

Chirpy smells. 'Soap?'

'No, love, an onion.'

She shivers and creeps under the blankets.

'It helps,' Dad says. 'I'll put it beside your bed.'

There's a silence, till Dad says 'That's what Mum used to do, when you had a cold ...'

Chirpy is afraid to move. He never talks about Mum. She hopes he's going to say something more, about things she used to do.

There is silence again, till Chirpy says 'Will you read to me?'

That's what Mum did so often; Chirpy remembers well.

'But it's the middle of the night,' Dad says, yawning.

Chirpy turns away.

'Oh well,' he says. 'OK. What shall I read?'

'About the bird that flew too far.'

And with a yawn and a sigh he begins to read.

When Chirpy sees him fall over with sleep, she'd like to say *Stay and lie down, for a while.*

But he stands up quickly, gives her a pat and goes to his room.

The onion helps. Chirpy doesn't wake up till eight o'clock. And there's no school – it's Queen's Day.

The sun shines off and on, but since Dad is at home too, Chirpy wants to go outside.

With the sun-hat and sunglasses in her hands, she hesitates for a long time, will she dare to wear them? She thinks of the dream, about the pit. What's that got to do with it? She waits no longer, puts the hat and glasses on, says 'Bye Dad,' and walks out of the house.

Behind the dark glasses and under the big hat, Chirpy feels wonderful. It's as if nobody sees her, while there are people everywhere, on their way to town.

Chirpy isn't going anywhere, just from one tree to the other. She's busy looking about, and when somebody waves to her, in the distance, she waves back.

The sun is strolling along. This time, he's not afraid to shine in her eyes. And Chirpy has such a bad cold that she's glad of the warmth.

'Hello madam!' she suddenly hears. 'The speedwell has been mown.'

Boldy comes cycling past, also on his way to town. He gets off and says 'You look like a mother, with that hat and those glasses.'

Chirpy feels so many things at the same time that she's confused. She says 'I want to be a mother who is not wise.'

'Why?' Boldy asks.

'Late in bed, never to school, ten babies ...'

'Oh,' says Boldy, 'then I'll marry you.'

'Alright.'

'So we'll have to make love,' Boldy says.

'Make love?'

'You know, cuddle up and things.'

'All right,' Chirpy says.

'But naked,' Boldy says.

'Oh.'

'Then you get babies.'

'Yes.'

'Do you want that?' Boldy asks.

'Babies, yes.'

'Are you coming to the fair?'

'To do what?'

'Go in the Waltzer.'

'No,' says Chirpy.

'And the merry-go-round?'

'No,' says Chirpy.

'Why not?'

'Makes me dizzy-go-round.'

Boldy laughs and says 'Good one! What about the horsetram?'

'What's that?'

'Just like a bus, but it's a carriage, pulled by horses.'

'And then?'

'You go for a ride along the old streets, with a coachman.'

Chirpy hesitates.

'It's free,' Boldy says. 'I always go twice. And I sit up front.'

Chirpy shakes her head.

'OK,' Boldy says. 'I *always* go alone. Cheerio!'

Running up, he jumps on his bike.

Then Chirpy says 'Cheerio.'

She goes to take a look at the mown speedwell, but it's such a sad sight that she goes back home.

Dad is busy in the garden.

'Can I help?' Chirpy asks.

He looks at her hat, looks at the sky, rubs his hair and says 'OK, the lawn needs raking. See all those brown leaves? From last autumn.'

They both work hard and when the lawn is finished, Chirpy asks 'Can I water the plants?'

'No thanks, I've just done them.'

'Oh,' Chirpy says. 'Let's go to the fair then.'

Dad bursts out laughing. 'The fair? What do you want to do there?'

'Go for a ride, in the horsetram.'

46

Dad looks at her without saying anything.

'It's free,' Chirpy says.

'But I was going to watch the tennis. There's a good match on this afternoon.'

'On the telly?' Chirpy asks.

'Yes.'

'*Again?*'

'Well,' Dad says, 'the tournament lasts a week.'

Chirpy stands right in the sunshine on the lawn and says 'Why don't you go and play tennis yourself!'

Dad is struck dumb. Then he starts laughing so loudly that Chirpy is confused again and says 'I'll go alone. Or with Boldy.'

'No,' Dad shouts. 'Wait!'

He runs after Chirpy, into the street.

'Who's Boldy?'

'You know, Baldwin.'

'Who's Baldwin?'

'Oh, my eh ... I don't know.'

'Is he in your class?'

'No.'

'Where does he live?'

'I don't know. We're going to marry.'

'Oh well,' Dad says, 'let's go to that horsetram first.'

The town is crowded but most people are near

the Ferris wheel and the roller-coaster.

A lot of children are on their father's shoulders. Chirpy would like that too.

The bustle makes her as shy as she used to be. And when she gets on the tram, she thinks where's Boldy?

There are other boys, much taller and wilder. There are also fathers and mothers, but Dad stays on the pavement, with his camera.

He waves and calls 'Say cheese!'

The big boys yell 'Say sex!' and they laugh their heads off.

Chirpy doesn't understand, but luckily she's in the front, near the horses, and there's so much to see, that soon she doesn't notice the boys.

In the evening Chirpy is exhausted. Never in her life, has she been out for so long on one day, certainly not on a sunny day.

She drags herself upstairs – stopping on each step – until she remembers something important.

On the same step as last night, she turns around and calls 'Daddy!'

He says 'What now?'

'I want *Mum* to put me to bed.'

Dad moans, closes his eyes and grabs at his head with both hands. 'Don't be ridiculous! We discussed that yesterday! Do you have a sunstroke or what? Stop whining and go to bed – it's eight o'clock!'

Sunstroke? Chirpy thinks.

Sunstroke? the sun thinks.

She stands up, takes hold of the bannisters and looks down on Dad, who's on the lowest step. His head is near her knees.

'And what if I *don't* go to bed?' Chirpy asks. 'Will you slap me?'

'Silly girl,' Dad says.

'Why not?' Chirpy says.

'Well, I don't need to, do I? What's got into you these days? Is it the flu or something?'

Chirpy says 'I *know* why you won't slap me ...'

'Oh?'

'Because you're scared! Because I'd hit back! Because now I'm taller than you!'

She doesn't move. She doesn't even blink. And it seems *Dad* is shy now, he coughs and scratches his chin. 'Oh, um ... OK.'

He doesn't even dare to look back.

'Now you must go to bed,' he goes on. 'Otherwise you really will be ill. Go and brush your teeth, I'll be up in a minute.'

Chirpy says 'I'd love Mum to put me to bed. *Please* ...'

Dad sits down on a step, with his back to her. He's leaning forwards, on his knees.

After a while he says 'Mum lives in a special house because she *can't* live here, I mean, she can't look after you.'

'Why?'

'Because it makes her so ... so nervous.'

'Why?' Chirpy asks.

'Because she's afraid she will fail. She's afraid that everyone is watching her, for example in the supermarket, waiting at the checkout – she might drop her shopping. And at home, in the kitchen, she's afraid there will be a fire when she's left the gas on, by accident. And she's afraid of the stairs ...'

Chirpy sits down too and says 'And of motorbikes. Or of a pit. Or shoot-soldiers ...'

'You know,' Dad says, 'sometimes Mum is afraid the sun will come down.'

Chirpy nods and thinks. 'Can you phone Mum?'

'No.'

'Can you go and see her?'

'Yes, I tried, but it doesn't help.'

'Then,' Chirpy says, 'you've got to write. Just write that she doesn't *need* to look after me.'

'And what about putting you to bed?'

'Oh, yes ...'

Now Chirpy is so tired that she climbs the stairs

on her bottom.

The sun has gone.

Dad is just as tired as Chirpy and both of them forget that she hasn't brushed her teeth.

Please stay and lie down for a while? Chirpy wants to ask, but she says 'You must write to Mum.'

'What about?' Dad asks.

'You know, about everything: the horsetram, and Boldy, and the speedwell, and Baby, and the motorbike and my pyjamas that you pulled at ...'

'Wait a minute,' Dad says. 'What baby?'

But Chirpy can only yawn now. She rolls over on her side and falls asleep.

She sleeps quietly, until her nose gets stuffed up again. Then she dreams about a stadium with a hundred thousand spectators. It's a football stadium, the largest in the world, but the pitch is empty. In the middle of that huge, empty pitch is Chirpy herself and the hundred thousand spectators are watching her! They're watching from all round, cheering, waving, shouting, singing, clapping for *her*, but the worst, the worst thing is the floodlights: Chirpy is caught in the biggest floodlights in the world. And she doesn't know why. Have all these people come to see her? What is she supposed to do? The lights are so fierce that they make her dizzy.

51

She screams.

'Chirpy!' Dad says. 'Don't! You'll wake the neighbours! What's wrong? Another nightmare?'

He sits on the edge of her bed, frowning. Chirpy covers her eyes with her hands.

'The lamp!' she says. 'You shouldn't switch the lamp on.'

Dad turns it off again.

They're both puzzled. Dad forgets to ask what Chirpy was dreaming about. He says 'You know, why don't you write to Mum yourself?'

'I can't,' Chirpy says.

'Yes you can. I asked your teacher and she says you can certainly write, if you *want* to.'

Chirpy nods.

'Well then ... You go back to sleep, have a good rest, and write a letter to Mum tomorrow.'

CHAPTER
SIX

Letters

TODAY CHIRPY almost enjoys school. She works so hard that the other children don't bother her. And as soon as she gets home, she goes on practising her writing.

When Dad comes home, he says 'Now you'd better play outside for a while, otherwise you won't sleep tonight.'

'But I haven't laid the table yet.'

'I'll do that,' he says.

Chirpy looks at him with round large eyes, without saying anything. Only when she goes outside, she says 'See you.'

First she runs into Baby. He's caught a young bird.

'No!' Chirpy says. 'That's not fair! It can't fly yet. And you get your food at home, don't you?'

Baby has the bird in his mouth. It's still alive, tweeting helplessly.

'Let go!' Chirpy says.

Baby looks round and drops the bird. It hurries into the bushes.

'Come and sit on my lap,' Chirpy says to Baby.

She sits on the edge of the pavement and he lets her stroke him.

When Boldy arrives, Chirpy says 'What a coincidence.'

'No,' he says, 'I was looking for you. Come and play tennis?'

'Tennis? Me?'

Giving her a racket, he says 'Piece of cake, just hit it.'

Baby gets off her lap and walks away.

'Don't catch any more birdies,' Chirpy calls after him. 'OK?'

She stands ready, with her racket, but the ball comes so fast that she misses it. Boldy serves again. Mishit. Boldy serves. Missed again. Boldy serves. Bad return.

'See?' Chirpy says. 'The racket is too big, I'm too small and the ball is too quick.'

Boldy laughs. 'Bad luck!'

'Anyway,' says Chirpy, 'I can write. Cheerio!'

'Hey,' Boldy calls. 'Wait. Come with me! I've got a nest with young blackbirds, fallen out of the tree, a real nest with living birds!'

Chirpy wavers. 'Tomorrow?'

'No, now.'

'Sorry,' Chirpy says. 'I want to write to my mother. Really sorry.'

'You want to be boss!' Boldy says.

'No, I don't.'

'Yes you do. You've ruined my day.'

Chirpy says 'I'm going home. See you tomorrow.'

The sun would like to come along, but dark clouds are in his way – *blast*.

They are big rainclouds – blackish grey. They hang over Chirpy's house. When the sun comes out once more, as if he's trying to push the clouds away, a rainbow appears, so clear and close, that Chirpy stands motionless.

Yes, the sun thinks, that's me. Take a good look, I'll be gone in a minute, damn, I can never stay! What a shame it's not a footpath, this bow of mine, a path of colours for the most beautiful journeys. Do climb it, come on – stay for a while – plenty of room – do anything you wish ...

The sun is gone. The rainbow is fading. It's like dusk.

For a moment it's perfectly still outside. The world is holding its breath. Not a leaf is moving. Then the rain begins to fall in large drops.

Chirpy would like to lie in the grass, it has this

nice smell ... She catches as many drops as she can, till she gets too wet. After that it's good to be warm indoors.

'Wash your hands,' Dad says. 'Dinner's ready. And look out, this pan is burning hot! You'll never guess what's in it.'

Chirpy takes off her wet coat, washes her hands, sits at the table and does something she's never done before, she tries to guess what's in the pans. Dad has warned they're hot, but he's still in the kitchen, taking off his apron, and he doesn't see that Chirpy touches a pan by accident – it's so close to her plate.

As if a knife has stabbed into her hand and another knife, another knife ... The stabbing doesn't stop.

She cries out and Dad says 'I warned you not to touch them! I didn't tell you without a reason! Let's have a look ... Come, quick, under the tap.'

He carries her to the kitchen, turns the tap full on and holds Chirpy's hand under the cold water.

She's screaming even louder, trying to kick herself free. When that doesn't help, she cries. 'Ow, don't, please don't! No ... I didn't do it on purpose ...'

Dad turns the tap off and stares at her. 'On purpose? Of *course* not, that's not the point. This isn't punishment! Oh, *now* I understand ... Do you hate the cold water so much? But you've burnt yourself! Look, a horrid mark, and the water helps, or else it would get worse.'

Chirpy is trembling and crying on the sink 'No, no, no ...'

Dad carries her back to the table. He fills a bowl with cold water and puts it in front of her.

'There, now you can put your hand in it yourself. Please try, then it won't hurt any longer. The cold soothes the burning, feel for yourself ...'

Slowly Chirpy lowers her hand into the water.

'See? Now hold it there quietly.'

It helps. She no longer feels the burning.

Dad takes an ice-cube from the fridge and puts it in the bowl.

'I wasn't angry,' he says. 'I just had to do something fast. And do you know what we're having?'

Chirpy shakes her head.

'Potatoes, green peas, mince and lots of gravy.'

Pointing to her hand in the water, he says 'Is it the hand you eat with?'

Chirpy laughs. 'No, I can eat.'

'Oh, good, or I'd have to feed you. Like a baby.'

For a while they eat without talking. Chirpy takes mouse-sized bites. Still trembling, she's afraid to drop the peas.

Dad says 'Are you going to write about this to Mum?'

Chirpy needs to think for some time. 'About the burning? Yes. Or else it's not fair. I was going to write *everything*.'

'Yes,' Dad says. 'How's your hand?'

'Fine.'

'I'm glad it's not the hand you write with.'

When Dad has finished his plate, Chirpy has a long way to go. She sees him wiggling his legs and she says 'You can leave the table, if you like.'

'OK,' Dad says. 'I'll start the dishes.'

As soon as Chirpy takes her hand out of the water, the sore starts throbbing again, so she asks Dad 'Please put my writing things ready.'

She has a pen and pink paper with white birds. He puts them beside the bowl with icy water.

A lot of the words Chirpy writes are wrong, but she doesn't know that and Dad doesn't mention it. She writes the words letter by letter, just the way they are said, and Mum will be able to read them perfectly.

'Dad?' Chirpy asks.

No answer.

'Dad?' Chirpy asks.

He's watching television.

'*Dad!*'

'Oh, sorry. What did you say?'

Chirpy says 'Is *finger* spelled with a long or a short g?'

'Oh, with a long one.'

Some time later: 'Dad?'

'Mmm?'

'Is *sorry* spelled with a soft or a hard s?'

'What?'

Chirpy shouts 'Stop day-dreaming!'

'Sorry, what's that again?'

'Is *sorry* spelled with a soft or a hard s?'

'Oh, with a soft one.'

On her way to bed, Chirpy stops on the stairs again. This time the sun can't watch or give a wink because the sky is full of clouds.

Chirpy turns round and says 'When I marry Boldy, you'll be my grandad, won't you?'

'No, I'd still be your father; I'd be the grandad of your children.'

Chirpy sits down and says 'Just perhaps, I might marry you.'

'Oh,' says Dad.

And Chirpy asks 'Could I?'

'Not really.'

'Why?'

'Because I'm your father.'

'But when I've grown up?' Chirpy asks.

'I'll still be your father.'

'No you won't,' Chirpy says. 'because you'll never be angry then.'

She gets up, climbs the rest of the stairs, brushes her teeth and gets into bed.

Come and stay with me for a while? she wants to ask, but she says 'My hand hurts and my nose is blocked.'

'Get some sleep first,' Dad says. 'That cures everything.'

But Chirpy can't sleep. She counts the dots on her pillow again, writes twenty more letters in her mind and imagines she plays tennis on television. Dad is watching, of course, and he sees her become a champion. She wins a golden cup, that is so big she can't carry it.

She wonders if Mum can watch telly in the Home? As long as she doesn't watch Newsround.

Chirpy gets out of bed to paint at her desk. The whole sheet of paper is turned into a rainbow, from her own house all the way to Mum's. The Home is in a park, with a pond, waterlilies, swans, a bridge, an appletree and a bench among the buttercups. She paints a dark sky and the raindrops are tears, but in a corner is the sun with big eyes, a broad mouth and long rays.

The paper is full and Chirpy is stiff with tiredness. She lays her head on the desk, just for a short rest, and when Dad goes to bed himself, at half past eleven, he sees that the light is still on in her room. Chirpy is snoring on her desk.

When he picks her up, she wakes a little and says 'So sorry, I was *just* going to bed.'

In bed she mumbles 'Are you going to the post-box?'

CHAPTER
SEVEN

That Helps

IN THE garden of Chirpy's house is a birch tree. When she looks outside this morning, there are still raindrops on the leaves and they are full of sunlight. It's like a fairy tree. What a pity the drops are falling off.

Chirpy wants to stay and watch this twinkling and falling all day long – there are millions of drops – but today is a normal school-day.

'Come on,' Dad says. 'Tomorrow is the weekend and Monday is a holiday – Liberation Day.'

Anyway, now that Chirpy is busy writing, she's beginning to enjoy school. Even at playtime she has pen and paper in her hand, and when the other children ask 'What are you doing?' she's not so shy.

At first she says 'Oh, nothing.'

More and more often she says 'I'm writing to my mother.'

And of course the children ask 'Why?'

'Because my mother lives in a Home.'

'Why?'

'Because she's *too* sweet.'

'Oh,' say the children. 'What are you writing?'

'Everything.'

'What do you mean?'

'Everything that happens, or what I like, or what I hate, and all the exciting things and the sad and pretty things ...'

'Like what?'

'Well, that I had this burn and that I've seen a rainbow.'

'Me too,' says an older boy. 'Who's for a game of marbles?'

They all are and Chirpy goes on writing. She writes that she'd like to have a go at a game of marbles – or perhaps just watch it for now – but she has something important to write: *Soldiers are dressed up men, so you don't need to be afraid of them.*

She adds that Boldy said it. Or else Mum won't know if it's real.

And you know: when somebody is being mean to me, I just tell him I do judo.

This afternoon Chirpy is looking for Boldy – because she likes him and because she's quite curious about the nest of blackbirds.

She doesn't even know where he lives, so she wanders about, behind the gardens, until she hears his voice, saying 'Don't you want any bread any more? OK, I'll eat it myself.'

She peeps from behind a shed – just a tiny bit shy.

Boldy is feeding the blackbirds. He sees her and whispers 'Ssh, they don't know you yet.'

He's sitting on the grass and the little birds are hopping around him.

'Too bad,' he says. 'They've just finished. Want a slice of bread?'

Boldy has a bag of bread left and they eat it together.

Chirpy reaches out with her hand. She'd like to stroke the birds, but they keep away.

'Because you're new,' Boldy says.

'How long will it take before they know me?' Chirpy asks.

'Oh, a week ... If you come every day ...'

'I'm not sure,' Chirpy says.

Over dinner, Chirpy asks Dad 'Have you really sent my letters off?'

'Of course.'

'In the post-box?'

'Yes, my love.'

'Why doesn't Mum write back?'

'I don't know. Perhaps she doesn't know *what* to write yet. Perhaps she's getting used to new feelings. She hasn't seen you for a long time, remember.'

'What's the colour of her eyes again?'

'The colour of the sea.'

'A bit blue and a bit green?' Chirpy says.

Dad nods.

'How long has Mum been in the Home now?'

'Five months.'

'Why don't you have a photo?'

Dad coughs. His eyes close for a moment and he says 'I *have* a photo.'

'Where?'

'In my desk upstairs.'

'Why can't I see it?'

'You can,' Dad says, 'but I didn't know if you wanted to.'

'Why?'

'I thought ... Maybe it would make you miss Mum.'

'I *do*. But not because of the photo!'

'I see.'

'Will you fetch the photo please?'

Dad pauses. Then he gets up and goes upstairs.

It's a long time before he comes back and when

he gives Chirpy the photo, he's shy.

She says 'Pretty, isn't she ... And not *too* sweet – just normal! Only one photo?'

'No,' Dad says. 'There are more.'

'Can I see them?'

Again he goes upstairs and now he comes back with a fat album. He hands it to Chirpy and makes for the kitchen, to start washing up.

She leafs through the whole book. It's full of photos of Mum and herself. Sometimes they make her laugh. Sometimes she cries – with longing.

'Can I have a frame?' she asks Dad.

'What do you mean?'

'A photo frame ...'

'I see. I ought to have one somewhere.'

'Two?' says Chirpy.

'I'll have a look tonight.'

'Do it now,' Chirpy says. 'That helps. And eh, make it three.'

'What do you mean "that helps"?'

'Well, if Mum is sort of here again ... it could be easier for her to come back ...'

Once more Dad goes upstairs and he gets Chirpy three frames. She chooses the best photos in the book and puts them in the frames: one on the table in the living room, one beside her bed and one in Dad's room.

Before going to bed, Chirpy looks out of the window in her room. The sun is a white ball, which doesn't make her eyes sting. On the other side of the house is another white ball in the sky: the moon, receiving its light from the sun.

Great, the sun thinks, when I leave, the moon is rising. The moon is surrounded by millions of stars and I haven't got *one*.

The sun is gone. The other side of the world is waking up. That's the way it goes, day in day out. The sun doesn't even know what a day *is*.

CHAPTER
EIGHT

Rainbow

IT'S SATURDAY and yet Dad is up as early as nine o'clock.

'Cup of tea?' he asks.

Chirpy nods and he gives her lots of milk and sugar.

After breakfast he asks as always 'Coming shopping?'

And today Chirpy says 'OK.'

In the supermarket she can steer the trolley.

'As long as you don't ride into the bottles of cola,' Dad says.

Chirpy is steering as well as she can and she's doing fine for a while, but taking a sharp bend, the trolley doesn't do as it's told. She doesn't hit the bottles of cola, she hits the bottom of a lady.

It was so fast that Chirpy doesn't exactly know what happened. She just sees a smart woman, who almost falls into the cola herself.

The lady turns and shrieks 'You wicked little chit! Who do you think you are?'

(A wicked little chit?)

'What do you think you're doing?'

(Gaping.)

'What's wrong with you? I'll *teach* you what's wrong! What kind of mother do you have? Don't stand there like a ninny, you ... you belong in a Home!'

At that moment Dad comes forward. His eyes turn dark. He takes a deep, snorting breath and stands right in front of the woman – as if he's pushing her over.

He says 'Well, madam, are you so terribly thirsty?'

She looks at him as if seeing a crocodile. Her mouth is wide open but no sound comes out.

Dad stays still too. He takes a bottle of cola, opens it in one quick movement and holds it above her head.

For a second it seems he'll empty the whole bottle, but after one dash, he stops, puts the cap on again, puts the cola into the trolley and says 'Are you coming, Chirp? Let's buy something special for tea.'

On their way to the checkout, he takes two

marzipan chocolate cakes and the biggest bag of crisps there is.

Chirpy looks back. The lady hasn't moved: her eyes are closed and her mouth is still open. One drop of cola is running down her forehead, over her nose. A group of people is watching her, as Chirpy and her father walk quietly out of the shop.

At home, Chirpy has a big glass of cola and as she's writing to Mum about what happened, the marzipan chocolate cake lasts nearly an hour.

'Is the post coming soon?' she asks.

Each day she expects a letter from Mum.

'Not just now,' Dad says.

'Oh, then I'll go outside for a while. Have you got a stamp? And an envelope?'

Dad writes the address and Chirpy seals the envelope.

'Are you going to the post-box now?'

'You know what,' Dad says, 'why don't you take it to the post-box yourself?'

'Will that help?' Chirpy asks.

'Who knows. And it's fun.'

She puts only her hat on and the sun is delighted – he follows her carefully.

Chirpy walks to the post-box. Nice colour. But how funny to leave your letter behind in there. Are letters ever lost? Do the postpeople take good care?

How she'd love to take the letter to Mum herself. But then you wouldn't *need* a letter, would you?

She holds it in the slit and says 'Have a good trip to the other side of the country ...'

She drops it. And hears it fall.

On her way back, she sees Boldy near his tree.

'Hello,' he says. 'All the blackbirds have flown away. Let's climb to the top ...'

He gets hold of the first branch and pulls his legs up.

Chirpy watches him climbing. She has to look higher and higher, against the sunlight. She takes a step forward, to stand in the shade.

'Coming then?' Boldy asks.

'No.'

'Why not?'

'I don't dare.'

'Pity,' Boldy says. 'You can see the whole country from up here.'

'No, you can't.'

'Oh well, *half* the country ...'

With a hand shading her eyes, Chirpy is staring upwards.

She asks 'Does anyone know how the world came about?'

'Came about?'

'I mean, how it was made, or something.'

'No,' Boldy says.

'Not even the government?'

'Nah ...'

'Or the hospital?' Chirpy asks.

'I don't think so.'

'If only the world doesn't die.'

'The world doesn't die by itself,' Boldy says. 'It's the people's doing!'

'Which people?'

'In factories and everything.'

'But,' says Chirpy, 'factories *make* things, don't they?'

'Yes, and *break* things ...'

'Like what?'

'The air. And the water.'

'Oh,' Chirpy says, 'we'll tell!'

'Who?'

'Well, the government or something. And my father. Do you know what he did to a lady?'

She tells about the cola and Boldy almost falls out of the tree with laughter.

Then he asks 'Let's play hide-and-seek. Or go and steal sweets?'

'No,' Chirpy says. 'The postman is coming.'

'So what?'

'There might be a letter from Mum.'

'From the Home?'

'Yes, I've written lots of letters now.'

'Good for you,' Boldy says. 'I've got binocs.'

Chirpy says 'Look out when you climb down.' And she goes home.

Near the frontdoor, with the rope in the letter-box, she hears a loud miaowing.

At once she knows that it's Baby and that he's frightened.

She walks toward the sound. It comes from the chestnut tree.

'Baby?'

He answers but she can't see him.

'You're not chasing birds are you? Are you afraid to come down? Do you want me to come up and help? I don't really dare ...'

Baby is crying so sadly that Chirpy gets worried.

'Do you want me to go and get Dad? Or would it be too late?'

His miaows are heart-breaking.

'What's happening?' Chirpy shouts. 'Must I help *now*? Must I try to climb up after all?'

She puts her hat down, takes a deep breath and reaches for the lowest branch, but at that very moment another branch is cracking, high in the tree.

Chirpy can't move with fear. Which is just as well, because Baby drops smack into her arms.

73

Chirpy falls too, on her hat, and Baby makes a bolt. He can't say 'Thank you'.

Chirpy does feel a pain – in her back – but the worst thing is the hat, it's all crushed and the rose has come off. She doesn't put it back on and the sun tries hard not to shine in her eyes.

You saved Baby's life, the sun would like to say. Better write to your Mum about that ...

Of course Chirpy will write about that.

She turns and sees Dad in the doorway. He's waving and calling and beckoning ... He's waiting for her!

'Post!' he calls. 'I was just coming to look for you. There's a letter for you, from Mum!'

He's holding a big envelope, with a beautiful stamp: a butterfly, and Chirpy's name is on the front, in large letters.

'For *me*?'

She's been waiting for a letter for days and now she can't believe it. Will it all be real?

'Come in, quick,' Dad says. 'Sit down at the table.'

It takes her ages to open the envelope, because it mustn't tear.

'Do you want me to help?' Dad asks. 'With my knife?'

Chirpy shakes her head.

Slowly she pulls a sheet of paper out of the envelope. It's a painting: a rainbow, a huge rainbow across the whole paper, and on each side is a house. Near one house somebody is waving, a girl. Near the other house, somebody is walking upwards, on the rainbow, right through the sun and clouds. This other person can't wave, because the bow is high and she's afraid to fall.

It's a long journey.

'If you fall,' Chirpy says, 'I'll catch you.'

'Pardon?' Dad says.

'Oh sorry, I was thinking.'

She watches Mum walking inch by inch on the bow of colours, from the other side of the country. The view is wonderful, but she looks straight ahead.

The sun is beaming. The whole paper is yellow with sunlight. Even the clouds are yellow-dark.

There's no letter. In a corner of the painting it says:

Dear Chirp, my girl, I miss you,
Mum.

Chirpy says 'I held Baby too.'

But this time Dad too is lost in his thoughts. He's staring at the rainbow, without hearing anything. He looks in front of him, without seeing anything. At least ...

Upstairs, Chirpy hangs the painting near the photo by her bed and for the rest of the day she's busy writing.

That evening she *almost* asks *will you stay and lie down for a while?*

She asks 'Why is your hair such a muddle?'

'My hair? Oh, it badly needs a cut.'

'Can I comb it?' Chirpy asks. 'I'm not sleepy at all.'

Dad looks at his watch. 'Alright ...'

He sits on the edge of her bed. Chirpy is behind him, brushing and combing his hair in all directions. Once she nearly touches his eye. So Dad shuts his eyes.

'Can I make little tails?' Chirpy asks.

'Tails?'

'Yes, like the dolls have.'

'Oh, fine.'

From the heads of all her dolls, Chirpy takes about twenty little hairbands: red, yellow, blue, pink and purple ones.

Dad's hair is not long enough, really. That's why she makes about twenty little dolls' tails at the back, on the sides and on top of his head.

It's a lot of work and Chirpy says 'Don't touch them!'

Dad feels his head, to find out what's happened to it.

'Oh well, all right.'

'Promise you will leave it like this!'

She thinks he's never looked so nice before.

Dad nods, puts her under the blankets, gives her a soft hug and goes downstairs.

A little later, the bell rings. Chirpy hears the front door and the visitor bursts into laughter.

Chirpy gets out of bed and walks down the stairs till she can look through the window over the door.

A man is laughing his heart out. Dad takes the bands out of his hair and combs it with his fingers.

Chirpy creeps back to her room.

Never mind, she thinks. Mum's got nice long hair. When she comes home, I'll make braids in hers.

Chirpy is still not sleepy. She draws the curtains back and leans on the window-sill. The sun has just gone. She forgot to wish him goodnight – there were *so* many things on her mind ...

The trees are now dark but above them, there is still some light. One bird is gliding up there. It has a white breast and it's flying so high that it shows the last sunrays, turning pink. How softly it's floating by.

As it fades from sight, Chirpy waves and calls 'Send my love! From me!'

CHAPTER
NINE

Not a Tough Man

IT'S SUNDAY and the first thing Chirpy thinks is no post today – pity. But surely the box will be *emptied*? And she begins her day with writing.

Then, while Dad is still asleep, she goes outside.

As soon as she arrives at the chestnut tree, Baby comes running up to her. He's purring and rubbing his head against her legs.

Chirpy kneels and holds him tight.

'Come and find Boldy?'

First they look near the speedwell. It's grown back nicely. Next, they walk to Boldy's garden.

He's built a big hut and a flag is blowing on the roof.

'Come on!' he says. 'This is a desert island and I'm the pirate. You know? A treasure island ...'

'What's the flag for?' Chirpy wants to know.

'For Remember Day, or something.'

'Remember Day?'

'Yes,' Boldy says, 'that's today.'

'Why?'

'Well, tomorrow the war was over, a long time ago, and today we have to think of all the dead in the war.'

'What war?' Chirpy asks.

'The Second World War. Are you coming now? The sea's over there, as far as the grass, and you are shipwrecked.'

'Where's Baby?' Chirpy asks.

'Gone. Drowned.'

'No, he's afraid of water.'

'OK, and you have to hide.'

Chirpy hides but Boldy finds her at once and locks her up in his ship.

She says 'When there's a war, I'll run to you and we'll hurry and sail to the desert island. Alright?'

'Alright,' Boldy says.

'But there won't be a war, will there?'

'Nah,' Boldy says. 'Anyway, when I'm sixteen, I'll move out and live on my own. With a dog.'

They listen to the wind.

Chirpy says 'When I'm sixteen, I'll get married *or* I'll take driving lessons, or else I can't go on holidays.'

'So when you marry me,' Boldy says, 'you won't need to take driving lessons.'

'Or I'll stay and live with Mum, for ever.'

'Is she back?'

'No. But I'll write and tell her I will live with her. If she'd like that.'

On her way back home, Chirpy sees more flags on the houses.

'Why don't we have a flag?' she asks Dad.

'I don't know, actually. Just laziness, I suppose. And I don't feel like it.'

'But it's for the dead!'

'Yes, I *think* of the dead ...'

Chirpy wants to ask how much a flag costs and if they're going to buy one tomorrow, but the phone rings.

Usually it's a boring conversation, about Dad's work or politics, and Chirpy never listens, but now there's an unfamiliar note to his voice.

Suddenly she needs to say something important, about Mum, but when Dad is on the phone, she's not allowed to disturb him.

She whispers into his ear 'Daddy ...'

He shakes his head and looks away.

'Can I say *one* thing, please?' Chirpy asks.

He pushes her aside.

Then it's too late, because Dad says 'Thank you,' and hangs up.

'Who was that?' Chirpy asks.

'Someone you don't know.'

'Who?'

'Mr Riders.'

'What was it about?'

'I can't tell. Let's play hide-and-seek.'

'Why can't you tell?' Chirpy asks.

'Because it's a secret.'

'Oh.'

She gets a funny feeling in her stomach. Dad looks nervous and that makes Chirpy feel nervous too.

'A nice secret?'

'I hope so. You have to be patient and don't ask about it again.'

'OK,' Chirpy says, 'let's play hide-and-seek. You go to the hall and count to one thousand.'

'Wait,' Dad says. 'First I have to go upstairs, to make some arrangements. You find a hiding place – I'll be there in a minute.'

Chirpy chooses a place that takes a lot of time and effort. She hides in the broom cupboard beside the kitchen sink. All huddled up, she just fits in, and she can't really move now, so the hardest part is to close the door. And it has to be left ajar, so she can see a part of the kitchen.

At first she's pleased with this place – Dad will never find it – but he's a long time trying. Her neck and knees are beginning to hurt.

Maybe Dad has fallen asleep upstairs. Or he's forgotten the time.

When she can't stick it much longer, she has to shout 'Are you coming?'

She doesn't hear anything, no voice, no footsteps on the stairs.

'Dad? Are you coming now?'

She doesn't hear anything.

'Dad! You have to come now!'

Everything hurts and everything is stuck – she can't come out or move at all. She can't call for help, nor cry, even her throat is blocked.

The sun is shining on the floor in front of the cupboard, unable to do anything for her.

Am I dying? Chirpy thinks. Or *have* I died?

She doesn't mind being dead, but she's so sorry for Mum. And for Dad.

'Chirpy?' she hears.

It sounds far away. It's a sweet voice, though. Is this heaven?

'Chirpy?'

She hears footsteps, more and more clearly, and the voice is also coming closer. 'Goodness, my Chirp has hidden so well that I'll never find her ...'

Yes you will! she wants to cry. In the kitchen! Let me out! I'm choking!

The sun wants to *do* something – it's so painful to watch and see helplessly. Keep it up, Chirp! I'm here, if that's any use. *Does* it help when I see you?

'Hey,' Dad says. 'How bright it is in the kitchen. And why is that cupboard door ajar? I'll just close it ...'

He tries to close it, but there's something in the way, something soft. 'Hey, what's this, what do I feel? A mouse? Has a mouse slipped inside? Rather big though. Or could it be a cat? Let's see ...'

Cautiously he opens the door. And gives a shriek. 'Chirpy? It's you! What a good place! I've been searching for hours!'

Chirpy can't say a word. Her eyes are shut too and *behind* her eyes are tears.

'Oh sweetie, what's wrong? Were you stuck? Here, Dad will help you ...'

That's not very easy. She can't even stand – her legs seem to be broken.

She starts to cry.

Dad is stroking her back and says 'Were you hiding all this time? I didn't know. You were hidden *too* well.'

'No,' Chirpy says, 'you were too late!'

'Um ... Yes. I forgot the time. And uh ... I'm sorry.'

So again there's a great deal to write about.

Chirpy takes an envelope and a stamp, writes the address neatly and asks Dad 'Are you coming to the post-box with me?'

He looks at his watch and says 'Alright.'

The sun is low now. Chirpy blinks, but she leaves the hat and glasses at home.

'Why are all the flags down?' Chirpy asks on the way.

'Because today we're not celebrating but commemorating. Tomorrow they'll be flying high – for Liberation Day.'

'About the war?'

'Yes.'

'But it was long ago, wasn't it?'

'Yes,' Dad says. 'Even before I was born.'

'And before Jesus and Mary?'

'No, that's even longer ago.'

'I see,' Chirpy says.

She's never talked so much before. She has to catch up for years and there are so many questions to ask. Are there any flags in heaven? Do trees like to rustle in the wind? Who made the sun? Will the sun go to heaven?

But Dad is not very fond of talking. At least, he forgets to answer. And Chirpy thinks I'll ask Mum.

In bed, she sees the sky turn purple and orange. The sun is setting behind the chestnut tree.

Dad says 'Sleep well.'

Chirpy looks at the sky and says 'Please stay and lie down for a while?'

'Me?' Dad asks.

He pauses and clears his throat. 'OK.'

Chirpy moves over.

As soon as Dad lies down, he's yawning. He huddles up and closes his eyes.

Chirpy asks 'Why did Boldy say "Second World War"? There's only one world, isn't there?'

'Yes, but there were two big wars.'

'Here?'

'Mainly in the rest of Europe.'

'But they'll never come back, will they?'

'No ...'

'Honest?'

'Yes, they are really over.'

'Or else,' Chirpy says, '*Mum* would be afraid to come back, see?'

Dad is silent.

'You know you're not so terribly tough,' Chirpy says.

She's looking at the last of the sunlight and asks 'When I'm eighty, will you still come and lie down with me?'

85

'Alright,' Dad says.

For a moment he seems to be falling asleep.
Then he gets up to draw the curtains.

'Leave them open,' Chirpy says.

'Will you be able to sleep then?'

She nods and Dad goes downstairs. Just in time,
because the telephone rings.

'See you tomorrow,' Chirpy says to the sun.

CHAPTER
TEN

At the Back of the Distance

DAD HAS a day off too, yet he doesn't sleep late. He takes a shower and washes his hair and Chirpy's hair.

'Put on some nice clothes,' he says.

He's never said that before, but Chirpy doesn't ask why. She puts on her blue dress and white lace socks.

'Let's buy a flag now,' she says.

'No Chirp, that's not so easy. A flag needs a solid holder. And I'm not sure if those shops are open today.'

'But it's Liberation Day.'

'Yes, which means that a lot of people won't be working.'

'And the post? Will there be post?'

'Well, to be honest, I don't know.'

Chirpy goes out to count the flags. When she's got as far as twelve, she sees Boldy lying under a bush in the park. She sits down beside him and asks 'What are you doing?'

'Look,' he says, 'a slug with a fat bum.'

The slug is sliding over a leaf.

'Do you dare to pick it up?' Boldy asks.

'No, you?'

'No. I'm not afraid, you know, but I don't dare.'

'Right,' says Chirpy. 'Because the slug doesn't *want* us to, I think.'

'Nice dress,' Boldy says out of the blue.

She looks at the sky and she'd like to say *Let's play princesses*.

Through a gap in the clouds, at the back of the distance, she sees the most beautiful blue of the world: soft and sunny.

For a while she forgets where she is. Then she says 'Is that the gate of heaven?'

Boldy looks too and says 'Yes, I think so.'

'But you can't see the dead.'

'Yes you can! The dead are just light, aren't they?'

'Yes,' Chirpy says. 'Comes with Remember Day, I suppose.'

Boldy gets up and says 'My flag is flying from the top. Wanna see?'

'No, I want a flag of my own.'

'OK. I could come and see yours tomorrow ...'

'Yes,' Chirpy says.

'OK. Cheerio.'

Chirpy tries to go on counting the flags, but all of a sudden she's restless and nervous – there's only one thing she wants now – to go home.

Outside the house she sees the postman and the moment he slips the post through her letter-box, she feels dizzy and sick. The postman walks on, and Chirpy has to stand still till the dizziness is over.

If I'm ill, she thinks, I can skip school tomorrow.

She'd like to run, but slowly she walks to the front door. The post is on the mat. She pulls the rope, closes the door behind her and picks up the letters. They are all for Dad, except one, which has her name on it. It's a small envelope, so there's no painting.

On a chair at the table, she opens it and reads:

Dear, sweet Chirp,

Thank you for all those letters. What adventures you had! And so many things you dare!

I can come home for a few days, to try and see how it goes. If it goes well, I can stay a while. Perhaps I'll come on Ascension Day, because you will have a holiday, I hope. What would you like to do? Or let's do nothing? I get so nervous when I think of it. Ascension Day is soon, isn't it?

Bye Chirpy, my Birdy,
Mum.

The phone rings. Chirpy is stuck to her chair. She's never answered the phone before. Where's Dad? Will he answer it upstairs?

The ringing goes on. It hurts her ears.

Chirpy goes towards the bookcase, where the telephone is. For one more moment she holds back. Just when she reaches out, the ringing stops.

In the silence, the toilet upstairs is flushed and she hears Dad open the door – too late.

If it's important, Dad always says, they will try again.

Chirpy sits down at the table and reads Mum's letter for the second time, for the third time and more times ...

Then she goes to show the letter to Dad. Reading it, he becomes very shy.

He says 'Well, make a list of nice things to do.'

'No,' Chirpy says, 'I'm going to buy a flag.'

'You can't,' Dad says.

'Yes I can, with my pocket money.'

'No, that's not the point. I checked, those shops aren't open today.'

'Then,' Chirpy says, 'I'll make a flag myself!'

'*Make* one?'

'Yes, with the rags from Mum's ragbag.'

She gets the sewing-box, finds a big needle and a big reel of cotton, then she goes to the attic and takes all the red, white and blue rags from the bag.

'But Chirp,' Dad says, 'that's too much work. You'll never make it!'

'Oh,' Chirpy says. 'Wanna help?'

'Me?'

'There's another big needle. When is Ascension?'

'Thursday,' Dad says.

'So we'll stay at home tomorrow, to work hard.'

Dad looks at his watch. 'Don't you want something to eat?'

'No, we have to clean the house and pick flowers ... Then Mum will *stay*, see? When *this* house is the best in the world, she won't need to go away again, ever.'

Dad looks at his watch. But Chirpy says 'Which colour?'

'Um, OK, I'll start with blue.'

'Then I'll do red.'

On the rug in the room, they put a few red and blue pieces together. The hardest thing is to make them fit, like a jigsaw, to cut as little as possible.

They are too busy to talk and eat, but in the afternoon, Chirpy says 'Are we having tea soon?'

'Yes, good idea.'

'With lots of biscuits or a fat piece of cake!'

'Oops,' Dad says, 'I'm not sure ...'

He looks in the cupboards and says 'I'm afraid ...'

The doorbell rings.

Dad doesn't move and he doesn't say a word. And Chirpy never answers the door.

'What's wrong?' she asks.

'I'm afraid we haven't got any cakes or biscuits left.'

'I mean,' Chirpy says, 'why don't you open the door?'

'Oh. Yes. The door. And eh ... Why don't *you* open the door?'

Chirpy takes a good look at him and says 'Are you *too* shy?'

'Yes,' Dad says.

'Alright.'

She opens the door to the hall, looks through the glass front door and whispers 'Mum ...'

She feels dizzy again and stops.

Mum is holding two bags and a big box and she's just waiting there. She can't even wave, only smile. Her whole face is smiling.

When the door is finally open, Mum says 'Hello Chirp, my love ... I didn't give you a fright, did I?'

Chirpy shakes her head.

Mum puts her things down and sits on the mat. Her letter was on the mat only that morning.

Is this real? Chirpy thinks. Is it Ascension now?

Mum says 'Come and sit on my lap.'

Chirpy snuggles up and closing her eyes, she says 'You're real.' And the newness of it all makes her tremble.

All she wants to do now is feel and smell and never let go again.

It lasts some time – Dad is still in the kitchen – but suddenly Chirpy jumps up. 'The flag! We haven't got a flag yet and no flowers and we haven't cleaned up ...'

'Well,' Mum says, 'I've been through a *real* disaster.'

She looks at the box she's brought and laughs – folds up with laughter.

Now Dad comes into the hall. He helps Mum scramble up and they hug each other till the end of time, till Chirpy says 'What about the box?'

'That was a cake,' Mum says. 'The biggest cream cake in the shop. And I dropped it. You know, when I got out of the cab.'

'In the *street*?' Chirpy says.

'Yes, on the pavement! Upside down! And a boy passed by and he stepped on top of it, I mean *into* it!'

'On purpose?'

'No, he was just walking there. I thought I was going to faint.'

'With laughing?' Chirpy says.

'No, with shame. But you know what the boy said? He said "You must be Chirpy's mother ..."'

'How did he know?' Dad asks.

'I told him,' Chirpy says. 'I told Boldy.'

'And you know what else he said? "You can borrow my flag." Then he picked up the box for me and walked on.'

'Well,' Chirpy says, 'we've almost finished our flag. Will you help us? And why did you write that you were coming on Ascension Day?'

'I *was*, but then I thought I'd better go right away, before Chirpy gets overtired, cleaning the house and everything. I did phone, but there was no answer. Fortunately, I brought a present I didn't drop. Come into the kitchen ... It's nothing fancy, mind ... Just saw it at the market. Here you are.'

Chirpy unwraps it: a little plant. True: nothing fancy.

'They will be yellow flowers,' Mum says. 'Look at the card.'

Chirpy sees the photo on the card and reads the name: 'Sun Child.'

She asks 'Will you stay till the flowers are out?'

Mum looks about the room.

She says 'Well, the flag isn't finished yet, we have to tidy up, pick flowers, bake a cake for tea, hug and chat ... How long do you think we'll need for that?'

'For ever,' Chirpy says.

Mum looks around again, leans on the table, closes her eyes for a minute, looks at Dad and from Dad to Chirpy and says 'Then I'll stay for ever.'

'Will the doctor let you?'

'He will if I want to,' Mum says.

'Oh, just phone him then.'

Tonight, the sun is so beautiful again: large, lilac, gliding – he's over the moon. He's going down, people say, because the earth is turning and turning ... It wouldn't be fair if one side were always light and the other dark.

So again and again the sun says goodbye to somebody who's going to sleep.

But I'm not *going down*, the sun thinks.

'Come and wave,' Chirpy says to Mum, who's putting her to bed.

They wave.

Chirpy is yawning. 'I'll write, to the other side of the world, and ask them to say good morning.'